GROUNDHOG DAY

NEWS

WILL WINTER
EVER END?

For Rachel and Sarah, who are more than just
one thing, and even more than they know —R. P.

For Mary Jane, Frances, and Henry —B. H.

First published in the United States of America in December 2015 by Bloomsbury Children's Books
www.bloomsbury.com

Bloomsbury is a registered trademark of Bloomsbury Publishing Plc

For information about permission to reproduce selections from this book, write to Permissions, Bloomsbury Children's Books, 1385 Broadway, New York, New York 10018
Bloomsbury books may be purchased for business or promotional use. For information on bulk purchases please contact Macmillan Corporate and Premium Sales Department at
specialmarkets@macmillan.com

Library of Congress Cataloging-in-Publication Data
Pearlman, Robb.
Groundhog's day off / by Robb Pearlman ; illustrated by Brett Helquist.
pages   cm
Summary: Tired of being asked only about the weather, a sensitive groundhog decides to take a vacation right before the big day in February.
ISBN 978-1-61963-289-9 (hardcover) · ISBN 978-1-61963-291-2 (e-book) · ISBN 978-1-61963-292-9 (e-PDF)
[1. Groundhog Day—Fiction. 2. Woodchuck—Fiction. 3. Humorous stories.] I. Helquist, Brett, illustrator. II. Title.
PZ7.1.P434Gr 2015   [E]—dc23   2014038764

Art created with acrylic and oil paint on watercolor paper · Typeset in ITC Legacy Sans Std · Book design by Amanda Bartlett · Hand lettering by Brett Helquist

Printed in China by Leo Paper Products, Heshan, Guangdong
1 3 5 7 9 10 8 6 4 2

All papers used by Bloomsbury Publishing, Inc., are natural, recyclable products made from wood grown in well-managed forests.
The manufacturing processes conform to the environmental regulations of the country of origin.

GROUNDHOG'S DAY OFF

ROBB PEARLMAN   illustrated by BRETT HELQUIST

BLOOMSBURY

NEW YORK LONDON NEW DELHI SYDNEY

Every year, on
one special day
in February,

Groundhog wakes
up *extra* early.

Crowds of people gather outside:
locals, tourists, even the mayor.
News reporters with large
microphones and big, shiny teeth
are waiting. Every year they ask
Groundhog the same things . . .

"Are there going to be six more weeks of winter?!"

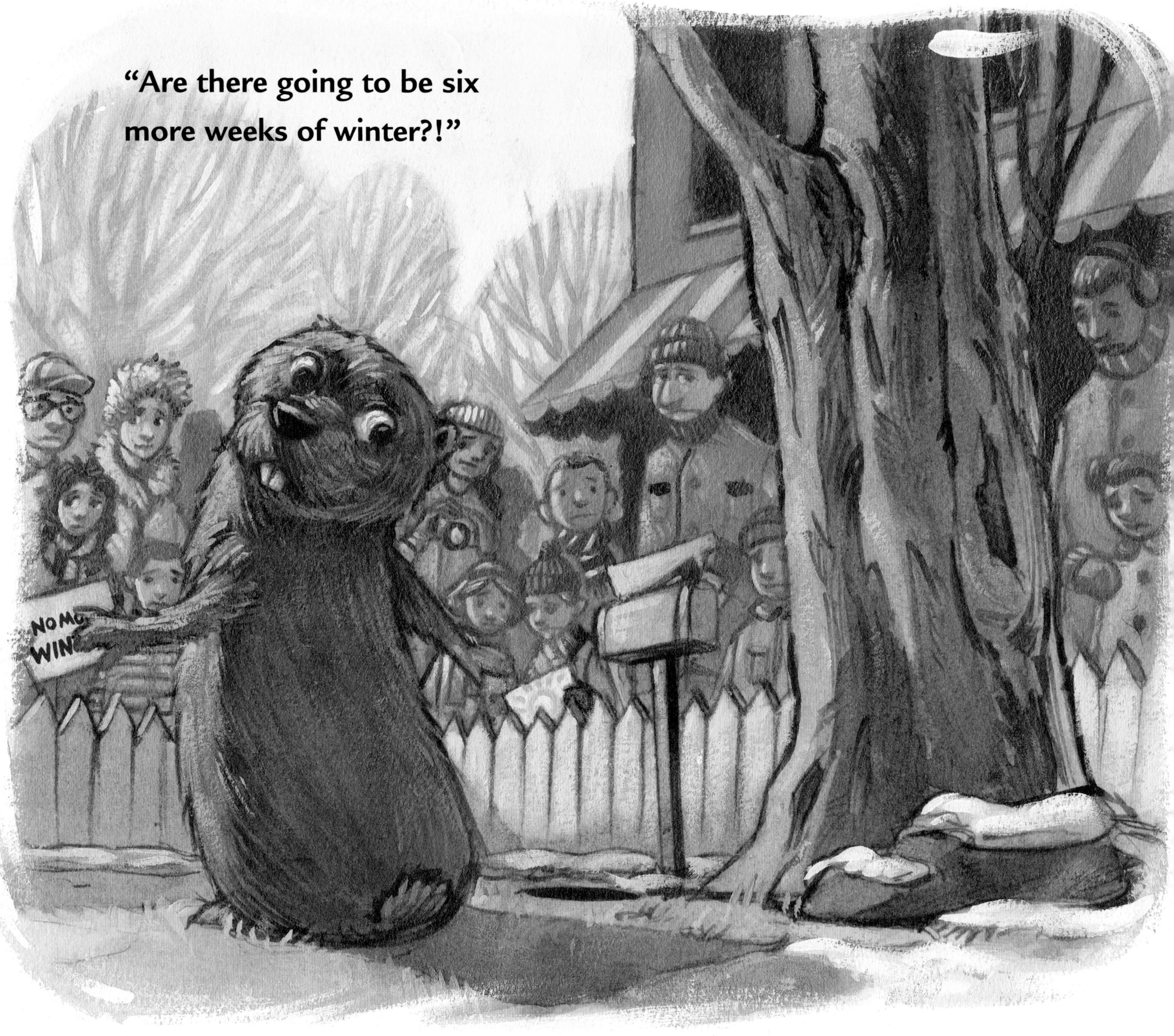

But the one thing they never ask Groundhog about is *him*.

No "How are you feeling?"

No "Have you seen any good movies lately?"

No "Do you like mushrooms on your pizza?"

Not even "Who does your fur?"

Groundhog has more to offer than the forecast. But that's what happens, year after year.

Well, not this year!

Dear People,

I am a groundhog with feelings and things to say! But all you care about is the weather. So this year I'm going on vacation. You'll have to find someone new.

Sincerely,
Groundhog

P.S. I'm taking my shadow with me.

Groundhog packed his robe, slippers, magazines,
and shadow . . . and headed for the spa.

The townspeople didn't know *what* to do. The mayor thought long and hard and finally announced, "We'll hold auditions for a new groundhog!"

Lots of animals wanted to try out for the role.

Elephant was just too big.

Ostrich got the whole thing backward.

Monkey was asked to leave after an unfortunate banana-cream-pie incident.

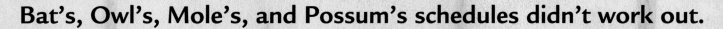

Bat's, Owl's, Mole's, and Possum's schedules didn't work out.

Poor Puppy suffered from stage fright.

And Sheldon . . . well, his shadow just wouldn't behave.

"This is terrible!" the mayor cried. "There's only one animal right for this job."

Groundhog had been relaxing when
he heard a news report.

"Nobody has Groundhog's flair for the dramatic!
Nobody can wake up as early as he does! No one," the
mayor said, pausing, "is as special as Groundhog."

Groundhog couldn't believe his ears. "They *do* think of me as more than just a weather vane!"

And with that, he threw on a towel and
whistled for a taxi. "Take me home!"

Groundhog tunneled
under the stage . . .

... and popped out of the hole!

TA~
DA!

The audience stood and cheered!

The reporters asked Groundhog all the questions he had always hoped they would ask.

"Where did you go on vacation?"

"Which team are you rooting for in the play-offs?"

"Do you prefer chunky or smooth peanut butter?"

"Is that your real fur?"

"Will you do this for *real* tomorrow?"

Groundhog stopped signing autographs. "*Tomorrow?*" he said.

The reporters nodded. "Tomorrow is Groundhog Day! You came back just in time."

"Well then, no time to talk! I have to go to bed early."

The next morning, Groundhog woke up *extra, extra* early. He poured himself a cup of warm mint tea and peeked out of his hole.

And *this* time, the reporters asked him about much more than the weather.

"What would we do without you?"

"Bagels or doughnuts?"

"What would you do
with a million dollars?"

"Seriously, is that your real fur?"

EXCLUSIVE

GROUNDHOG TELLS ALL!

"You like me, you really like me!" Groundhog said with a huge smile. He finally felt like everyone cared about him. He was very happy.

That is, until he climbed back down into his hole . . .

. . . turned on the television . . .

and saw that Bunny had hopped away.

Auditions would be held in the spring.

I QUIT